For Thomas, my brother

Library of Congress Cataloging-in-Publication Data available.
ISBN: 978-0-8118-7547-9

Book design by Amelia May Anderson.
Typeset in Handwritten.
The illustrations in this book were rendered with pen and watercolor.

Manufactured by C&C Offset, Longgang, Shenzhen, China, in February 2011.

10 9 8 7 6 5 4 3 2 1

This product conforms to CPSIA 2008.

Chronicle Books LLC
680 Second Street, San Francisco, California 94107

www.chroniclekids.com

Paul Hoppe

chronicle books · san francisco

Every night before bed, I turn on my night-light, read a story, curl up under a blanket, and give my bunny a hug. But last night, I couldn't find my bunny anywhere!

There was only one place left to look.

I had to go into the Woods.

And I wasn't afraid at all. Until . . .

I ran into a BIG, SCARY BROWN BEAR!

HONEY

But the bear was just afraid of the dark.

So I shared my night-light with him.

Then the big brown bear followed me
deeper into the Woods.

And we weren't afraid at all. Until . . .

We ran into TWO SCARY GIANTS!

But the giants were just bored.
So I shared my bedtime story with them.

Then the giants and the big brown bear
followed me deeper into the Woods.

And we weren't afraid at all. Until . . .

We ran into a SCARY, FIRE-BREATHING TRIPLE-HEADED DRAGON!

But the dragon just had a stomachache.

So I gave him a hug.

Then the fire-breathing triple-headed dragon, the giants, and the big brown bear followed me deeper into the Woods.

And we weren't afraid at all. Until . . .

We came to a big, spooky, dark cave.
At first, nobody wanted to go in.

But we took each other by the hand
and marched into the dark together.

And we ran into a

VERY BIG,

HAIRY, SCARY

MONSTER!

He had something furry
in his hand.

I asked him, "Why did you take my bunny?"

"Because I'm lonely all by myself in this big, spooky, dark cave," said the very big, hairy, scary monster.

"Why don't you come back with us then?
We'll all share my bunny!"

So we did.

And we were not afraid at all.